MW01142222

By Charlotte Blood Smith

©2015 by Charlotte Blood Smith

Published by: Slaughter Mountain Publishing Company

Cover Design/Layout: Rita Durrett

Interior Design: Rita Durrett at www.RitaDurrett.com

This book is a work of fiction. Names, characters, places, and incidents are fictitious or used fictitiously. Any resemblance to real persons, living or dead, to factual events or to businesses is coincidental and unintentional.

PRINTED IN THE UNITED STATES OF AMERICA

Table of Content

A New Rope

She adjusted the black veil and head piece, frowning as she examined the results in the mirror. Good thing she had remembered Mama's black voile dress. It had been worth the search through all the trunks in the attic. Nowhere in this town to buy proper fabric to make a real veil.

Satisfied she stepped back. Now she looked like a proper follower of the Profit. He would be pleased the next time he saw her. His eyes were blue and she wished hers were too as she felt that would have been another connection between them. At least they both had gray hair. She could hardly wait for his next visit which wasn't scheduled for another two weeks. She would have so much to tell him.

A satisfied smile crossed her face. She could never thank the Almighty Power enough for bringing Rafael to her. All those years she had wasted! Her anger rose anew. All those people who had lied to her had led her to believe for a time that Christianity was the true religion. Now they even refused to take her name off the membership roll of that church. That snippy secretary. Telling her it wasn't something she could do. She could use an eraser, couldn't she?

At least she had been lucky enough to find out before it was too late, she comforted herself. Now there were other things she needed to take care of. Those liars weren't going to get away with threatening her and spreading this blasphemy any further.

Agatha slipped a claw hammer and large butcher knife into the deep pockets of her voluminous black skirt. The knife had to be returned to Ellen. So careless, leaving it at the park after the church watermelon feed. True Believers didn't keep things she reminded herself, even if the real owner did just leave it where anybody could pick it up.

How could she have fallen for those lies all those years? And how had she been lucky enough to sit next to the Profit the last time she had taken the bus into the city? He had been so helpful, taking the time to come back up every weekend for the last month, patiently explaining how a woman who was a True Believer would conduct her life, how she should dress, what the Almighty Power would expect of her. She consoled herself with these thoughts as she strode rapidly toward the main part of town, leaving puzzled friends looking after her as she swept by without speaking contrary to her usual habit of talking to everyone.

"What do you want with twenty-feet of rope," Harry asked as he prepared to cut the length from the coil at the back of his hardware store.

"That's none of your business and a man that was a True Believer wouldn't speak to an unmarried woman in public," Agatha replied stiffly as she counted out the correct amount to the penny before slipping the coil of rope over her arm and stalking out, distracting from her haughty exit by stumbling at the threshold as the veil obscured her sight of the slight step down to the sidewalk.

Now what kind of a tangent has she gone off on this time, Harry wondered as he watched Agatha sail out of the store looking more like a vulture than a human with her black garments flapping around her. At least her crazy ideas were always harmless he assured himself. She did appear to be more intense this time than usual. Before she had never chewed him out for speaking to her.

First step accomplished she thought, heart pounding slightly with anticipation as she entered the residential part of town, her rapid progress causing her attire to billow around her like the sail of a pirate ship.

Where to start, she wondered? Momentary panic set in. What if they weren't either one home or there was someone with them? They were together so much. She remembered all the times she had been the third person in the trio. Clear back to grade school they had always been together, Ellen, Jerri and

Agatha, everybody knew that. Until she learned the truth; until they turned against her, threatened her. Refused to listen to her when she tried to tell them this marvelous truth she had learned.

Her steps quickened as she turned down the alley behind a row of houses. Arriving at the third gate, she eased it open and stopped, staring for a moment at the woman stretched out face down on an air mattress at the side of her pool apparently asleep.

How dare she tell me I needed a bath! Agatha crept closer, footsteps silent on the thick mat of grass. Telling me she had to roll the car window down because of the smell, which everybody in town was talking about it. Standing over the still sleeping figure she withdrew the hammer bringing it down on the back of the sleeper's head. Swiftly she struck three hard blows before grabbing the edge of the air mattress and rolling her into the pool pitching the now bloody hammer after her.

"There Jerri," she whispered. "You think so much of baths. Take a good, long soak."

Silent as before, she slipped back through the gate and hurried farther down the alley, a grotesque black bird in the summer's heat. As if for reassurance, she adjusted the coil of rope over her shoulder and touched the handle of the knife, now alone in her pocket before opening the back gate of the house two doors down from Jerri's.

"Would you like a glass of lemonade?" Ellen asked the hunched black figure perched on a stool in her kitchen. "You look hot in all that get-up. At least I think you'd be if I could really see you. And why on earth are you carrying that rope?"

"I believe I could use a drink, a real cold one." Agatha pushed the veil back and slid off the stool as Ellen turned her back and reached into the refrigerator for the pitcher of lemonade. Swift as a snake striking she closed the short distance between then and drove the knife between Ellen's shoulder blades.

Waiting only until Ellen was stretched out on the floor she tied a hangman's knot in the rope, pausing to listen for a second to the sound of a siren on Main Street before placing the loop around Ellen's neck.

"Telling me I ought to be hung with a new rope just because I complained about how things are done in this town will you," she muttered as she completed the job and turned, coil in hand searching for something over which to drape the remainder of the rope.

"What the hell is going on here?" Police Chief Chad Bingham demanded as he jerked the front door open and crossed the room with long strides. "Agatha, what have you done?"

"I had to first."

"What do you mean, first?" Bingham asked as he knelt beside Ellen feeling in vain for a pulse "what do you mean had to?"

"Jerri was going to give me a bath. She's so fond of baths I decided to let her take a long one, but you got here so quick you've messed things up. Why are you here? You're always at the Buckhorn drinking coffee this time of day?"

"Jerri has neighbors who have two-story houses.

You were seen and they called me. Why, Agatha? They were your best friends since we were kids."

"Well, Ellen was going to hang me with a new rope so I had to do it first."

"But you didn't hang her, you knifed her." He indicated the knife still protruding from her back.

"It was her knife. I had to return it didn't I? I couldn't keep something that wasn't mine. That would be a crime."

An Ill Wind

Lt. Kelso flipped his notebook shut and glanced at the victim whose expression still registered both shock and anger. This was the third burglary in as many nights in the upper class Big Cedar addition of Martinville. Prime area, he thought, all those big groves of cedar trees which gave the area its name and provided one of the selling points for the area; privacy. The woods and rolling hills made it impossible for any house to be visible to its neighbor.

A badly splintered front door showed how entry had been made. No need to worry about being heard way out here, Kelso thought. Left a burglar free to do whatever it took to get in. He frowned studying the area around the door.

"Was the alarm set?"

The victim ran his hand through his hair already mussed from previous assaults.

"I don't have one. I thought out away from town like this there would be no problems. One of the reasons we built out here, supposed to be nice and quiet. Crime free," he added.

"I'm afraid there is no such thing as a crime free area anymore," Kelso replied. "I guess that's all I need. You'll bring the list of what was taken down to us tomorrow?"

The victim shrugged in resignation.

"Yeah, I'll bring it down. Fat lot of good it'll do."

"Don't give up. We do recover stolen property now and then," but not nearly often enough he reminded himself. "This is the third house in the area that's been hit in the last week. You really should put in a burglar alarm."

Kelso opened the door and stepped into the night pulling his coat collar up against the cold wind. It had begun to sleet since he had gone indoors, needle sharp little pellets of ice against which the wind whipped trees provided little protection. If this storm had hit earlier the victim would probably have been home rather than at the opera. Not much chance of anybody being out in weather like this to notice what was going on at a neighbors. At the sound of the victim's voice he glanced back.

"You're probably right. Guess I'll give that alarm salesman a call. Shouldn't have to, supposed to be crime free out here," he continued as he shut the door.

Kelso looked up as Sgt. Laramie laid a stack of typed statements and reports on his desk.

"Here's the lot. All three owners, the neighbor who saw a van pull out of one of the driveways and the officer's reports."

"Thanks. There is just too much coincidence for these not to be the work of the same person. All three were hit too close together and all after it had been in the paper the owners were planning to attend some civic function that night. Maybe if I read everything straight through I'll find the connection."

"Hope so. Well crime is calling so I guess I'd better answer," and with a wave of his hand Laramie left, summoned by not one but two phones ringing.

Kelso was soon engrossed in the statements, jotting down notes to himself as he went through each one and then checking to see if the items that had caught his eye in one appeared in any of the others. There were several items which showed up in more than one report that continued to bother him. Why had the victims built houses that expensive and failed to install a security system? Before he could follow that thought with any action, Laramie stuck his head in the door.

"Sorry to interrupt, but I think you'll want to hear this."

"What now?"

"I had an officer go to every house in that subdivision and see how many had security systems and how many had turned down a chance to purchase one. When he got to that place that's on the cul-de-sac at the end of the road he rang the doorbell and when nobody answered he knocked on the door. The car was in the drive. When he knocked the door swung open and when he looked inside there was a man lying on the floor. Head was split open apparently with a bronze football trophy. Looks like the storm must have sent someone home early last night."

"How bad was he hurt?"

"Bad enough. He's still out and the doctors are acting worried. I've got an officer at the hospital in case he wakes up and can tell us something."

"Are the uniforms still out there?" Kelso asked as he grabbed his overcoat off the rack by the door and fell in behind Laramie's rapidly moving figure.

Laramie nodded.

"Find any witnesses?" Kelso asked the officer busy searching the area around the car.

"No, Sir. Snow pretty well took care of that, but he had taken his keys and locked the car so I don't guess he saw anybody before he got in the house."

"Probably right."

A thorough search of the house indicated a number of things had been taken including the wallet of the owner, who the medical examiner identified as being a local pharmacist.

By the time Kelso had finished at the latest crime scene and returned to the police station the day was almost gone. Skimming through the notes he had been working on when he was interrupted he completed his earlier plans and reached for the phone.

"Mr. Carlson? Sorry to bother you, but this is Lt. Kelso. No, we haven't caught the burglars yet, but maybe you can help me do just that. I can't help but wonder; why didn't you have a security system installed when you built your house?"

"They advertised the area as crime free. We just didn't see any reason to, but you can bet we're going to now."

"What do you mean, advertised as crime free?"

"That's what the ad said. Live in a crime free area. One of the reasons we bought here. We were so tired of crime in the city. Been broken into five times in the last six months we lived there. So tired of it. Thought the country was different. Should have listened to the burglary alarm salesman instead of believing the ad."

Expressing his thanks for the help, Kelso hung up. Rapidly he telephoned the other victims only to be told essentially the same thing. All had felt secure primarily because of the way the ad had been worded.

"Where was this ad everybody keeps talking about?"

"It was the whole front page of that special real estate section the paper puts out each spring. All about getting away from the crime in the city and moving to a crime free area. I guess I should have listened to the burglar alarm salesman who called me the other day instead of the ad. He was right when he said there wasn't any such thing as a crime free area."

At the second mention of a recent call from a

burglary alarm salesman, Kelso snapped to attention.

"I'm afraid I'm going to have to agree with him. Do you know what company he was from?"

"Sure. Wrote it down. Have it right here. It's called Catch A. Thief Alarms. Address is 500 S. Main. Said if I called back in less than twenty-four hours I'd get a twenty-five percent discount. Should have listened to him. Now I'm going to have to pay full price on top of what I've lost."

"Thanks."

Briefly Kelso wondered about anyone advertising an area as crime free. However, a quick check with the company that had built the addition brought the information the owner at the time the ad had run had recently died of a heart attack after discovering his own home burglarized. Apparently he hadn't been the one to place the ad and the woman who answered the phone at the paper said whoever it was paid cash so they had no record.

On that bit of less than helpful information he hung up and called the Chamber of Commerce. Its records showed To Catch a Thief had only been in business a couple of months, but was located in one of the higher rent districts. Business must be good, Kelso thought. Might as well go check them out. Goodness knows, I don't have anything else to go on at the moment. Maybe if one of their guards had been in the area one of the nights a burglary had occurred he would have seen something.

Making a right turn off a busy street, Kelso

braked to a stop and crawled out of his unmarked car gazing with interest at the white van parked in the To Catch A Thief parking lot. On the side, under the name of the company, was a black silhouette of a robot placing handcuffs on a masked burglar. Wondering why the door was standing open on such a cold day, he entered to be greeted by a company employee, a small man, about thirty, wearing white coveralls with the company logo on the back. He hastily closed the door to another room as he caught sight of Kelso.

"Help you?"

"I hope so. I understand you have some customers in the Big Cedar Addition and wondering if you might have had a patrol there any of the last three nights?"

"Why?"

"I'm sorry. Guess I should have identified myself," As he reached for his badge he was treated to the sight of the breeze from outside slowly swinging open the door to the room the man had just closed revealing an assortment of microwaves, TVs, guns and, sitting on a desk a gold statue whose description exactly matched one he had been given while investigating the preceding night's burglary. On the wall was a copy of the ad he had heard so much about.

"I do believe you're going to be an even bigger help than I thought," he continued showing his badge as he informed the man he was under arrest and began to recite the Miranda.

"You have the right to remain silent. Anything you say can and will be used against you. You have the right-----'"

"What the hell are you talking about?" he demanded as Kelso started the warning. Following Kelso's gaze he jerked his head around and also saw the now open door which had been the cause of Kelso's sudden change of expression from fatigue to joy. With a sigh he slumped against the counter, all resistance gone.

"It always amazes me how the criminal mind works," Laramie said. "When I was booking our friend he was complaining this wasn't how things were supposed to be. Said nobody should suspect someone in the burglar alarm business of being a burglar since everybody knew they were in the business of catching thieves. How did you tumble to it?"

The two were in Kelso's office wrapping up the final details of the case. The suspect was enjoying the hospitality of the county pending his first court appearance and most of the reports were ready to present to the district attorney the following morning.

Kelso laughed.

"I know what you mean. When I read back over the reports I noticed each victim said he had been contacted the day before the burglary by a salesman wanting to sell him a security system. I went a little farther and called the others in the addition. Almost all of them had received similar calls all from the same company. The ones hit had turned the salesman down. The others either bought or told the caller they already had alarms. I still wasn't sure until I saw the van and it matched the neighbor's description, white van with some hind of black logo. I knew I had the right man, but I probably would never have been able to prove it if the breeze hadn't blown the door open while I was standing right in front of it. As the old saying goes, it's an ill wind that blows nobody some good."

Community Help Line

Earl Schroeder rubbed the back of his neck as he replaced the telephone in its cradle. His shift at the Community Help Line was coming to an end and he was anxious to have it over with. Tonight had been too routine, nothing you could really get excited about. He liked the nights where there was a real crisis to deal with. As his hand left the receiver the telephone rang again.

"This is Help Line. Can I help you?"

"I hope so," a halting voice whispered.

Schroeder leaned back and relaxed. The undertone of panic in the voice reaching his ear told him this was going to be the monotony breaking call he had been wishing for.

"Could you tell me what the problem is?" he asked, quickly engaging the voice scrambling device while kicking himself that he hadn't turned it on before he answered. Drawing the telephone log closer, he filled in 4:25 a.m.

"Please tell me."

"I just can't take much more."

"Are you in danger right now?"

Schroeder strained to listen as the voice dropped lower.

"Not right now, he's gone."

Schroeder relaxed again.

"When will he be back?

"About six. I don't know where he goes, but he always stays gone till about six on Tuesday morning."

Schroeder took a sip of coffee. Try and get a name and telephone number. This was one of the first instructions given during the training sessions for this position.

"Can you tell me your name and phone number where I can call you back if we get cut off?"

"Ellen."

Schroeder gripped the phone harder. "A number?"

"Oh, no! I don't think I better do that. He might answer when you called."

"Then I'll just hang up."

"That would make it worse," she said, the note of panic increasing. "Every time someone hangs up he says it's one of my boy friends."

A slow smile crossed his features.

"So, you have boyfriends?"

"No, on no, I'd never do that! No man would

want me anyhow. I know because he tells me so all the time and he's a man so he should know. He just stays because he doesn't believe in divorce."

Schroeder's voice conveyed sympathy across the telephone lines.

"Did something happen today?"

"Yes."

"Would you like to tell me more about what happened?"

The pause lasted so long he thought for a minute he had lost her.

"Yes, I think I'd like that."

Schroeder fished a cigarette out of his pocket and struck one of the kitchen matches he favored on the underside of the desk, cupping the flame as he puffed. "

"Well, it goes back quite a ways. When we first got married, that was ten years ago, everything was fine. We had such fun together." She paused, apparently reliving the good days.

Impatient, Schroeder interrupted her. "Go on."

"Of course he got mad at times, I mean, how could he help it, married to someone as dumb as I am, but then he'd say he was sorry and we'd make up and he'd be so sweet for a while." She sighed again. "The last few years it hasn't been that way at all."

Schroeder leaned back and propped his feet on the desk. Now it was getting to the interesting part. These women usually followed the same pattern. At first everything was rather vague, but after a few questions they got down to facts.

"How did it change?"

Remember your training, he cautioned himself. Always ask questions that require more than a one-word answer.

"First he just got mad now and then, but now he blows up all the time at nothing."

She began to cry. Schroeder shifted the receiver to his other ear and reached for the coffee pot to replenish his cup. They always started to cry somewhere during their recital.

"Nothing I do is right," she continued, sobs hanging in her throat. "Just nothing. Do you have any idea how hard that is to live with?"

"Ellen, can you give me an example?"

"So many. Just tonight he got mad because I didn't keep his dinner warm and he tried to push my head into the garbage disposal and it was running. My hair got caught and it pulled a hunk out. Last night he hit me because I did try to keep it warm and he said it was too dried out to eat. Accused me of trying to poison him."

"Why do you need to keep his dinner warm?"

He listened, fingers drumming rapidly on the tabletop, as she tried to control a new burst of sobbing. He couldn't believe what he was hearing. His own wife telling someone she thought was a stranger about him! Lies and more lies! Like he was the one in the wrong. With a huge effort he focused again on what she was saying, trying his best not to give her any indication as to who she was really talking to.

"Because he never comes home at the same

time, but he expects me to have dinner ready when he walks through the door. Last night he was three hours late."

Schroeder rose and walked the length of the room, almost knocking the coffee pot off the end table as he made an abrupt turn. By this time in nearly every interview he was always so charged up he had to pace the floor to release some of the tension. This one tonight was turning out to be one of the best in a long time. No, the very best ever.

"Has he hurt you bad enough to need medical treatment?"

Again he listened to sobs.

"I only went to the doctor once. I had to; he broke my leg when he pushed me down the stairs. He got even madder then. Said it was my fault for being so clumsy. Said my leg wouldn't have broken if I hadn't tried to get away, had stood there and taken my whipping like a wife is supposed to." She paused. "All the other times I just took care of myself. Not much a doctor can do for a bruise. He got so mad because of what the doctor charged for setting my leg. Told me if I ever cost him another bill like that the next one I ran up would be my funeral bill."

Schroeder nearly burned the end of his nose as he lit another cigarette, hands shaking with excitement.

"Has he ever hurt you in any way except by beating?"

She sobbed again.

"Yes, he burns me."

"Did I understand you right? He burns you?"

"Yes, with his cigarettes. He'll put them out by grinding them into my leg or back."

Schroeder dropped the cigarette and ran a shaking hand through his thinning hair. This was the best one he had had in a long time. Probably the best he would ever have since he had recognized her voice.

"Does anyone know how you're being treated? Have you told your family? Do you have any friends you could go to?"

Be careful, he cautioned himself. Too many questions too close together might cause her to hang up.

"Nobody knows. My family doesn't live here and all I have left anyway is an aunt and some cousins I haven't seen since our wedding. He never would let me go to visit them and finally they stopped asking."

"What about friends? Surely they've noticed the bruises?"

"I don't have any real friends. A long time ago we used to visit with some of the guys he went to school with and their wives, but we stopped. He always accused me of coming on to them."

"Were you?"

"No. I just wanted somebody to talk to."

"Did they ever see the bruises?"

"Oh, no! He's always real careful. He never hits me where it has to show. He beats on my back and stomach or on my head where my hair will cover it up. I can't let anyone see. That's why I wear long sleeves in hot weather. To cover up the marks on my arms." She sighed. "I guess what I really should have been was an actress. I've had lots of experience keeping people from finding out."

"Why don't you want them to know?"

"Well, it's pretty embarrassing for people to know you're so dumb you cause your husband to act like that. Besides, he'd lose his job and then where would we be?"

Schroeder ran two fingers around the inside of his collar, pulling on it as if it was choking him.

"What is his job?"

"He's a preacher."

Schroeder's eyes lit up. Good she still hadn't recognized who she was talking to.

"Have you tried to leave him?"

She sighed again, the sobs now a thing of the past.

"Once."

"Why did you go back?" He asked lighting still another cigarette even though half of the previous one was burning in the ashtray.

"Lawyers want money to file a divorce and I didn't have any or anywhere to go. He sees to it I never have any money. Not even enough for a bus ticket anywhere or a motel room for the night."

Schroeder inhaled deeply then crushed the cigarette out scattering butts and ashes across the desk. Without looking he brushed the mess onto the floor.

"What did he do when you went back?"

"Beat me. Beat me bad. I think I had a concussion, everything was blurred for a day or two. I told everyone I had the flu."

"Have you ever called the police?"

"Oh, no, that would just make it worse. They can't do anything. If he had to pay a fine or go to jail he would be even madder than when he had to pay the doctor. Don't you see, there isn't any way out. Not any."

Her voice slid away into a whisper.

"No way out. No way."

"You could let us help you. If you'll tell me where you are I can have a policeman pick you up and take your to a safe house."

"Do you think I should?"

Schroeder hesitated. He knew they had been cautioned not to make up the person's mind for them. Just to do the extensive questioning so they would have to look at the whole picture. He listened to her soft sobs start again and knew he had to answer the question somehow.

"Nobody deserves to be beaten."

"Are you sure? Nobody ever said that to me before. He always tells me I deserve what I get because I'm so dumb and keep doing dumb things he can't stand. He's real smart. He has a doctorate."

After a pause he asked, "The address?"

"No, not just yet, but thank you for listening. There's one more thing I haven't tried. You know the Bible says, 'till death do us part'. I'll just have to work this out myself."

The line went dead.

Schroeder unlocked the door of his apartment

pushing it back with unnecessary force and increasing the force even more as he slammed it shut.

"Ellen, where are you? How could you be so disloyal? Talking to a stranger about us and lying about me. You know I've told you never to do that. What a man and his wife do in their own home is their business. Ellen! Where are you?"

At a double click behind him he spun around.

"What do you think you're doing!"

"What you said. Getting out. I recognized your voice when you answered. You're right, nobody deserves to be beaten" and then she pulled both triggers. Her look of satisfaction was the opposite of his of stunned surprise.

Cupid Killed Them

"I just thought you might like to see them before we moved them, Chief."

"Right Williams, glad you called me. Okay, pick them up."

At the Chief's order the ambulance attendants move toward the car. Wedged in the front seat were two people, a man and a woman, both obviously dead.

Now the finding of two dead people, even two dead people in a car, was not sufficiently unusual in a town the size of Wright City to warrant calling in the Chief of Police at 7:30 in the morning to view them personally, but this case was a little different.

In the first place, the man must have weighed at

least three hundred fifty pounds and was stuck solidly in the front seat. He appeared to be forty-five to fifty and stark naked. All he had on were his socks. There was no visible cause of death.

By contrast the arms of the woman protruding from underneath on each side were small and bird-like. The average person could have circled her wrist with thumb and forefinger and had one joint left over. Her arms, one foot and her hair were all that were visible as the ambulance attendants started to remove the bodies.

"Looks like they've been dead quite a while," Williams said.

"Yeah, he's been dead a lot longer that she has," the Chief remarked. "Rigor mortis has set in pretty good in him, but her arm's still limp. Who found them?"

"Mr. Jameson over there," Williams replied gesturing toward a small, nervous acting man standing near the rear door of a store. "Found them when he started to open his store this morning. Guess they've been here since Saturday night. Store's closed on Sunday."

After a considerable struggle, the ambulance attendants, assisted by two uniformed officers, succeeded in removing the man. Well over six feet tall and at least three hundred and fifty pounds besides being stiff, his removal had been an experience not likely to be forgotten soon by those involved.

The Chief and Williams moved in for a closer look at the woman. Also naked, slightly built, about thirty-five-years-old, maybe one hundred pounds, about five feet tall; she immediately brought to mind a spider which had been smashed. Removing her from the car was no problem and in a few minutes the ambulance was on its way with its uneven human cargo.

Back in his office, Williams had just finished filling out his report and pushed it back to await the autopsy report when the phone rang.

"Williams."

"Say, want to hear a good one?" The voice was that of the county medical examiner, Dr. Casey Breed.

"Sure, shoot."

"Well, you know that pair of stiffs your boys brought me this morning? By the way, that's a lovely way to start a Monday morning. Well, anyway, I think I've found probable cause of death. First, the guy weighed three hundred and fifty-four pounds and the girl ninety-seven. Now, get this. He died of a heart attack, probably about 11 p.m. Saturday. Rigor was starting to go out so that means he had been dead between twenty-four and thirty-six hours. She died of suffocation about five this morning. Rigor just starting so she had probably been dead bout three hours. Just couldn't move him I guess. On the report for cause of death I could put, Cupid Killed Them?'

"Yeah, I guess you could," Williams replied and hung up to the sound of Breed laughing at his own joke.

Suspicion Pays My Bills

"That's my report. All I can do is tell you what I see. I can't change what he does."

Amanda Stone looked again at the report I had handed her. On it in careful detail was a list of her husband's activities covering the past twenty-four hours.

"He went from his home to his office, ate lunch at the Stockade with a man from his building, went back to work, to the gym for a workout after work, by his mother's house and home. I've lost five pounds following him to his workouts to make sure he doesn't meet someone there and gotten a lot of strange looks from some of the men. They seem to think pumping iron a strange activity for a woman."

"Yes, I see the problem, but I know there's another woman somewhere. I just can't figure out why we can't locate her."

I leaned back enjoying the comfort of the sofa. After all the hours I spent sitting in a car it felt good to relax on a really good sofa.

"Why are you so sure there's another woman? I've been following him for a month now and every day reads just about like that one. You tell me he doesn't go anywhere without you on the weekends or after he gets home. Personally, I think you're wasting your money."

I watched Amanda take a fast turn around the room. She was getting frustrated at not being able to find that woman. Some people find it hard to adjust to the fact that just because they have money doesn't mean they can get what they want instantly.

"I can tell by the way he treats me. He acts like he's trying to make up for something just like he has all the other times. It's my money. If I want to waste it that's my business, not yours," she snapped.

"Okay. Just voicing my opinion. I've spent longer on this case than I ever have before without turning up anything. Did you ever get proof of the other affairs you said he's had?"

"I never tried."

"Then how do you know he was running around?"

"I can tell, and "how" is my business."

Getting back in my car I though over all that had transpired. I had accepted the job just over a month ago after a former client had recommended me to

Mrs. Stone. Henry Stone was a corporate lawyer with a thriving business, but the real money in the family lay with her. Her father founded the law firm and Henry started as a junior partner marrying into his partnership. When her father died Henry had become head of the firm, but she inherited all of the stocks, bonds, trusts and other money making ventures he had been involved in.

She said her suspicions had been aroused when she came by the office and was told Henry was in court. Since she had just come from the court house and been informed court had recessed, because the judge had suddenly become ill, she had started looking for Henry, to no avail.

Fuel had been added to the fire when an acquaintance remarked about seeing Henry getting into a car with a woman with long, dark hair.

Satisfied I hadn't given myself away anywhere I headed for Stone's office building. Today was one of his days to go straight home, but just in case she decided to check and make sure I was doing what I was being paid to do, I parked across the street from the main entrance and settled down to wait. Right on cue, Stone waked from the door to his car and drove out of the parking lot in the direction of his home. I would be home early tonight.

"Are you sure you went everywhere he did this week?"

"Well, except for the restroom and I can't follow him from office to office in the building. He might get curious as to why I was there."

"Maybe I would have been ahead to hire a man, he could go anywhere. Maybe he spotted you. Knows he's being followed."

"I don't think so. I keep changing my hair color, style, and as you can see from my expense account I rent a different car every day. He doesn't act like he knows he's being followed. Acts like a man going about his business with nothing to hide."

"Damn it! I know he's hiding something and I'm sure it's another woman."

Amanda picked up the pile of reports, by now quiet thick, and started through them.

"You bring these in every Friday morning. Maybe he's gotten on to when you're not out there and that's when he meets her. From now on very it, bring them in the afternoon part of the time."

"All right, but I still think you're barking up the wrong tree."

"I'll decide what tree to bark up. You just do your job."

"Fine with me. Easiest money I ever made."

This case had proved to be like having a steady job. No more parking in front of massage parlors till four a.m. waiting to get a picture of some would-be Romeo emerging. Stone didn't kept late hours, he never left the house alone after he came home. It was just too good to last. Even the most jealous wife should be convinced after this long.

"At last you've come up with something. I just wish you'd gotten a picture." Amanda was almost smiling as she looked at my report. "He met her Friday for lunch, you say in the report. Where were they?"

"That little French place over on Third. He didn't pick her up, just met her there, ate, and left alone. I couldn't get close enough to hear what was said, just close enough to see they were together. For all I know they could have been talking business."

"Describe her again."

"Small, about five feet one or two, blond, cut short, one hundred and ten pounds all in the right places, possibly thirty."

"At least he isn't fooling around with some teen-ager, but I don't buy that business angle. If it was for business why didn't she go to his office?"

"I tried to follow her, but another car stalled in front of me just as she pulled out of the parking lot and I couldn't get close enough to even get the li-cense number."

"At least now you'll have to admit I was right."

"I suppose so."

I had to congratulate myself. That blond should keep me employed at least another month. Then I'd have to come up with something else. Jobs like this hadn't been too prevalent since I resigned as a meter maid and opened my own detective agency.

"He seems to be getting careless. You say he picked his blond up and took her to the Coachman Inn for lunch?"

"That's what happened. She came walking up to his car in the lot just as he came out of the building. They drove out of there, spent two hours, and came back. She went into the building with him, but must have gone out the side door. Anyway, I never did see her come back out and when he came out, as usual he headed for home."

"You didn't follow them into the Inn?"

"You can't get in there without a reservation, and since I didn't know that was where he was going to take her, I had failed to make one."

"You don't have to be sarcastic. He's getting careless. Surely before too long you can find out who she is."

"I'll keep trying. At least now I know what I'm looking for. Of course she could wear a wig or he could change girlfriends."

Things rocked on for a little while and then Mrs. Stone began to get demanding again.

"I know it seems like he's having all the luck. How was I to know they would close the intersection for a parade just after he went thought with his blond with him? All I could do was sit there. It was a pretty good parade, elephants and everything."

"I'm not paying you to watch parades. I'm paying you to get some sound evidence I can use in court. Now see if you can do it or I may look for somebody else to finish the job. I'm beginning to think I should have hired a man."

All the way home I turned the possibilities over in my mind. When I got there I still hadn't arrived at any decision. I put the rented car in the slot that went with my apartment, I don't own a car and she is paying the bill so I don't turn it in every day, and took the elevator to my apartment. A hot shower sounded better to me than anything. I had worn the red wig today when I took in my report to show her just how hard it would be to recognize me. She almost didn't let me in when she first opened the door, which got my point across, but the thing made my head itch. As I was pulling my sweater over my head I head the click of the front door lock.

"Honey, you here?" Henry called as he pushed the door shut.

"Yes, in the bedroom."

As I threw the sweater on a chair and unzipped my jeans Henry Stone appeared in the doorway.

How'd thing go?"

"Not the best. She's threatening to get some-body else if I don't come up with something concrete pretty soon. She says she should have hired a man in the first place so he could have followed you to the rest room."

"I don't know why she would think I would have a woman hidden in the men's room."

At the absurdity of this though they grinned at each other.

"We'll think of something. This is too good to loose. She pays you wages so you don't have to work and I don't have to worry about her following me be-cause she thinks you are. That adds up to some of the best afternoons I've ever spent."

"Yes," I agreed, "that's all we have to do. You could say suspicion pays my bills."

"Not any more. As of now you're out of a job."

The blast of the shotgun was followed by Henry's collapse.

"He should have been watching to see if someone was really following him. Didn't take much to catch the door before it locked."

With that Amanda backed out the door and I frantically dialed 911.

Terminal Treatment

Detective Sherry Palmer replaced her cell phone in its holster and turned towards the worried looking man standing about five feet away.

"That was the cardiac care unit. He didn't make it."

Dr. Cliff Evans shrugged. "I didn't much think he was going to. He could have been unconscious for up to twenty minutes before he was found and that's a long time for a heart to be stopped."

The patient in question hadn't been in surgery or undergoing any other treatment that should have been life threatening. He had been in the physical therapy unit recovering from a car wreck in which his vehicle had been struck on the driver's side resulting in him being knocked sideways then jerked back by the seat belt. This had caused every muscle in his back to be severely stressed. The hot packs and electrical stimulation were being administered along with ultrasound to relieve the soreness. Exercises were being used to stop muscle cramps and spasms and reduce trauma to the area. Neither the accident, which had happened three weeks ago, nor the treatment should have been life threatening.

"It appears to have been a heart attack, but since we don't know for sure we'll need to take a better look around and talk to the people directly involved in the treatment."

"Just let me know who you want to talk to."

"Let's start with the therapist that was working on him last."

"I think he had left to do a home health visit. One of the techs would have done the ultrasound and hooked him up to the e-stim." Evans turned and looked towards the corner of the gym where several of the techs were huddled together. "Which one of you did the ultrasound and hooked up Mr. Rowe to the heat and e-stim?"

There was a brief pause and a small, blond headed girl stepped forward.

"I hooked him up."

"What's your name and had you treated him before?" Palmer asked.

"My name's Beth, Beth Collins, and yes I hooked him up Monday and Wednesday. He just started treatments this week."

"Once their treatment plan is worked out the therapist usually guides them through the exercise part and the techs do the e-stim, hot or cold packs and the ultrasound," Evans said. "Everybody here at City Memorial Hospital works together; the doctor, therapist and technicians. We have a complete treatment program following an accident or surgery if needed."

"Are you the doctor in charge of the rehab facility?" Palmer asked Evans.

"Yes."

"Was there anything wrong with, let's see, Elbert Rowe, is that correct, in addition to the results of the car wreck?"

"Yes, he had two very severe heart attacks, the last one about three months ago," Evans said. "But a simple hot pack and e-stim treatment shouldn't have caused any problems."

Palmer turned towards the girl that was visibly shaking.

"How long have you worked here?"

"About three months. I got out of school in May."

Would you please walk me through what happened between the time you took Mr. Rowe to the room and when you left?"

"I let the table down so he could get on it without me having to help him. I'd already brought the hot packs in and put them on the chair. I had him lie down on the table and did the ultrasound first. He was lying on his stomach and when I got that done I put the electrodes and leads on his back; two on each side of his spine, one on each side about the middle of the shoulder blade and the other two about six inches below that. Then, since he was on his stomach, I put the hot packs on over the leads, punched in the time for each one, turned out the light out and walked out. When I went back in, he was dead."

Beth began to shake even harder and then to cry. "I didn't look at him as I left."

"Did he say anything to you before you left?"

"Only when he first laid down."

"Had anything else happened in relation to Mr. Rowe being treated before today, if you know? "

Beth ducked her head again, "yes."

"What was that?"

"Every time I went in the room with him he made a lot of remarks I didn't like."

"What had happened or been said by either of you when he said these things?"

Beth stood with her eyes downcast and hands clasping and unclasping for a few seconds.

"I told him I didn't appreciate what he said." she said.

"What had he said?"

"He was very rude and every time I took him into the treatment room he would ask me if I wanted to get up on the table with him and let him give me a "treatment". Today when I started the ultrasound he reached over and grabbed the inside of my leg."

"What did you do?"

"Well, the first time I just said "no" and the next time I said "no way" and today I just backed up as far as I could and finished the treatment."

"Why didn't you tell me this was going on," Dr. Evans asked.

"I didn't want to talk about it. I thought he would stop when I didn't do what he wanted."

"Have you had trouble with any other clients?" Palmer asked.

"No, just him."

As Beth subsided into silence one of the crime scene squad came out of the treatment room carrying the lead wires and pads that connected the e-stim machine to the patient.

"Think you might want to take a look at these," he said, handing them to Palmer.

She took the wires and began to examine them from one end to the other. Stopping at the patient end of two of them, she looked up at Evans.

"Would it be normal for there to be scorched areas on the pads?" she asked.

With a startled jerk, Evans moved closer and looked at the area Palmer was indicating.

"Never," he said. "Those are used with wet packs. We make sure the connections are tight. Water getting in might cause a short."

"I think it probably did," said Palmer. She turned and looked again at Beth, who by this time had sunk down onto an exercise mat and covered her face with her hands. "Would you like to tell me what really happened?"

For a short time Beth continued to hide her face and cry. Finally she slowly raised tear filled eyes to

Palmer and said, "Yes."

"Go ahead when you're ready."

"I knew him a long time ago. When I was ten he was our PE teacher at school. One day he told me to wait when the bell rang and as soon as the other kids were out the door he grabbed me, took me in his office and raped me. He told me if I told anybody they wouldn't believe me and he would kill me. School was almost out and he did it every day for that last week. We moved that summer and I hadn't seen him since, but I recognized him immediately. I don't think he recognized me, but I wasn't sure he wouldn't and I didn't know any other way."

"It probably wouldn't have worked if he hadn't had a bad heart," Evans said. "I just wish you had told me or someone as soon as you recognized him." Evans continued to look at Beth. "You said he didn't say anything after you started treatment."

"That's right."

"Just where were you using the ultrasound?"

"On his shoulders and neck."

"Just where on his neck?"

Beth shrank even farther into herself, looking only at the floor.

"Just where?"

"On his shoulders and up each side of his neck."

Evans shook his head. "Don't you know not to use ultrasound over the carotid arteries?"

"Yes, but it was the only thing I knew might make him be still long enough for me to get the e-stim hooked up. I was afraid he would want to know why I

43

was putting a wet towel over the connections since I hadn't before. I just couldn't stand for him to touch me again."

Evans shook his head. "If you had just told me none of this would have happened."

"You have to come with me," Palmer said. "I too wish you had told someone. It might have made a big difference in how this finally turns out."

Gently Palmer put her arm around Beth's shoulders and led her from the room followed by the crime scene officers carrying the e-stem machine and the incriminating wires and pads. The sound of her crying was abruptly cut off by the closing of the door.

The Box

"Hurry up, Elizabeth. I've waited forty years for this opportunity." Hester spoke over her shoulder to her sister who was getting out of the funeral home limousine. As soon as Elizabeth was clear of the door the funeral home director shut it and drove away, completely ignored by the two old ladies as they hurried toward the front door.

Dressed in black, one short and fat, the other taller than average and thin almost to the point of grotesqueness, they resembled a couple of birds of prey descending upon a corpse.

"Will you hurry?" Hester, the thin one snapped.

"I'm hurrying, I'm hurrying. If it's waited for forty years it'll wait a few minutes longer."

As Hester inserted her key in the front door a

45

squad car pulled to the curb. Two men, one in plain clothes, one in uniform, studied the two figures for a minute before the plain clothes man gave a sign of resignation and climbed out.

"Pardon me, ladies, which one of you is Mrs. Cletus Clagg?"

Hester turned with a look of impatience.

"I am. Who wants to know?"

The officer suppressed a smile before introducing himself.

"I'm Lt. Wright, homicide. I'm here to inform you you're under arrest for the murder of your husband, Cletus Clagg. It is also my duty to inform you that you have the right to remain silent and, should you choose not to, anything you say may and could be used against you in a court of law."

"Well, I never! Now who would come up with that fool notion? Me? Murder Cletus? We were married for forty years."

"Some might think that was sufficient reason," Wright replied.

"What makes you think he was murdered?" Elisabeth asked faintly. "He died of a heart attack. The doctor said so. Said he was surprised he lived as long as he did the shape his heart was in."

"The autopsy says the heart attach was brought on by a massive overdoes of digitalis, enough to kill someone with a good heart."

Both ladies became silent. First they looked at Wright. Then they exchanged a long look. Finally Hester shrugged and continued to open the door which was half open when Wright announced his errand.

"Where do you think you're going?" he asked Hester as she stepped through the door.

"In the house of course. People with manners don't discuss their personal business standing on the step where every Tom, Dick and Harry can hear them."

Again canceling a grin, Wright followed the two into the front parlor. Now few houses in this age of ranch style and McMansions have a front parlor, but the room into which they stepped could be described only in this manner. The furniture was from another age, massive, dark and most of all plentiful. In the middle of the clutter was a wooden pedestal on which sat an ornately carved wooden box. About eighteen inches square, it was dominated by a large, brass lock.

Hester placed her handbag on the arm of the sofa and withdrew a manila envelope. Opening it she unceremoniously dumped its content on the end table and began rummaging through what had obviously been the contents of a man's pocket.

"Isn't it there?" Elizabeth hovered behind Hester trying to get a look at the pile of belongings.

Hester scooted aside the billfold, watch, glasses case, nail clippers and pocket knife without so much as a glace. Like a vulture who has spotted his prey she swooped down on the key ring. Among the usual house, car and suitcase keys one stood out; a large, brass key. Holding this up with a look of triumph she turned toward the box.

"What are you going to do?" Write asked.

Hester looked at him as thought she had forgotten he existed.

"Open this box, of course."

"Wait a minute. What's in it?"

She turned to face Wright with the attitude usually reserved for explaining things to small children or mental defectives and began to enlighten him.

"If I knew what was in that box I wouldn't have to open it. For forty years I was married to Cletus. For that whole forty years I had to dust that box. It always had to have a place of prominence in the room and people were continually asking me what was in it, but I could never answer that question. For that whole forty years he refused to tell me. The only time I came close to finding out was one night I woke up and he wasn't in bed. He hadn't been feeling well so I got up to see if he was all right. He was down here. Just as I came down the stairs and got to where I could see around the door he finished putting something back in the box and locked it. Now, you may lock me up for the rest of my life on some fool notion I gave him two much medicine, but before you do I'm going to find out what's in that box!"

Taking Wright's silence as acceptance for her plan of action, Hester again turned toward the box key in hand. In the silence which emphasized Elisabeth's rapid breathing, Hester turned the key. With the faint click of a well-oiled piece of machinery the lock opened. Hester lifted the lid and slowly withdrew an ornate brass urn.

With one accord Elizabeth and Wright pressed forward to read the inscription on the plate on the urn's side. In stunned silence the three read, "Herein lie the ashes of my beloved wife, Sarah."

Although Hester appeared thunderstruck neither she nor Wright was prepared for the effect this revelation had on Elizabeth. With a wail as though suddenly bereaved she collapsed on the rug.

This collapse galvanized Hester into action. In a minute she whipped a bottle of smelling salts out of her purse and waved them under the nose of her sister. Choking, Elizabeth regained consciousness and struggled to sit up.

"Oh if I had only known," she wailed. "If only I'd know it wouldn't have been necessary."

Interrupting her sister's wails, Hester assumed her usual attitude of command and demanded an explanation for such behavior.

"Would you be so kind as to explain yourself? Going off into a fit as if a ghost had just raised up out of that box instead of a jug of fifty-year-old ashes and in front of strangers."

Wright again made his presence known with a question.

"What did you mean, if you'd known it wouldn't have been necessary?"

"Why, if I'd known all along all that was in that box was ashes I wouldn't of had to kill him. The way he guarded it I thought it was money or something really valuable and I wanted to be sure Hester got it. All he could talk about these last few weeks was going to Lass Vega and living it up. You see, he was sick anyhow. I just helped him along."

"I agree, straight to the graveyard. Better get you things. We need to go see the district attorney and then get the name changed on this warrant."

Struck speechless for possibly the first time in her life, Hester watched the possession of Elizabeth, Wright and the uniformed officer move towards the police car and didn't even think to close the door against the winter cold.

Thou Shall Kill Not

I knew even before I answered the telephone what the call was about. It had only been two weeks since I moved to Morganville and not too many people knew I was here. Being the pastor of a small church in a small town I really wouldn't get that many calls, even after I had been in town long enough to get acquainted. I had already been invited to dinner by most of the families in the church so the call likely pertained to the other primary reason a pastor was called; a death.

"Rev. Wells? This is Marsha Walker. I don't know if you've heard, but my grandfather, Amos Walker, was found dead this morning. Someone killed him."

I listened to her tearful account of what the police had told her. The old man had been hit in the back of the head with a blunt instrument. I had met him at church the first Sunday I was here. He was in his late 70s, living alone on a small pension, apparently well-liked by his neighbors and obviously not well off, a strange candidate for murder.

I hung up after promising to come by the house later in the day to discuss the funeral arraignments. This would have to be on a tentative basis as it was not know at this time when the police would release the body.

When I arrived at the home of Miss Walker and her parents, I found among those present an investigator for the district attorney's office.

"Rev. Wells, I'd like you to meet Len Craner," Mrs. Walker said as she introduced me. "Len is the investigator for the district attorney's office and he's trying to figure out what happened to Grandpa."

"Pleased to meet you," Craner said as he shook hands. "You're new in town aren't you?"

"Moved here two weeks ago," I told him. "Was over at Centerville for a couple of years before that."

Craner said the body would be released the next day so the family and I went ahead and completed plans to hold the funeral in three days.

The next morning I had just arrived at the office when Craner knocked on the door.

"Come in. What can I do for you?"

Craner sat down across the desk from me. He laid a folder on the desk and leaned back as though he intended to stay awhile. Made me just a little nervous, but why should I worry?

"You told me yesterday you came here from Centerville, didn't you?"

"Yes, I was there for two years; pastor of the Central Church."

"Do you remember a Willis Jordan?"

"As a matter fact I do. Preached his funeral the first week I was pastor. He was chairman of the committee that hired me. Seemed like a nice man. Sorry I didn't get to know him better."

"Before that where were you pastor?"

"Coopertown."

"There about two years?"

"Yes. Our convention rotates us every two or three years most of the time."

"And before that?"

"A little place up in the north part of the state called Cedar Grove. Why do you want to know where I've lived?"

"A funny thing came to my attention last night. I was talking to a friend from over at Centerville and he mentioned hearing on the news about the killing. I told him the preacher that was going to preach the funeral was from Centerville and asked him if he knew you. He said he did, not personally, but he remembered your name because you preached the funeral of a friend of his that was killed about the same way two years ago."

"What is your friend's name? Maybe I know him."

"That's not important. I asked him exactly how his friend was killed. Then I got to thinking and called some people over there and found out where you had been before Centerville. They told me and I made some more calls. I called clear back to Cedar Grove. That was the first church you went to after you graduated from seminary, wasn't it?"

"Yes, I went from there to Cedar Grove, but I still don't understand why you are so interested in what I've been doing?"

"Because it struck me funny that twice in a row you would be called on to preach the funeral of a murdered man within days of moving to a new community. It seems as though that wasn't enough of a coincidence. I found out this had happened in every church you've gone to. And another funny thing, none of the killers have been caught and in each instance it was a man who was well liked, not rich, but a pillar of the church you were pastoring. Now, I probably should read you your rights before I ask the next question. Doesn't all this seem a little strange to you?"

"Not really," he said. "There is no better way to get acquainted in a new church than preaching the funeral of one of the more active, long-time members. Anyway, it has always worked for me."

Total Kill

There were signs of murder everywhere. Just inside the door of the small house in the middle of the block. I had to step over two just to get inside. There were more bodies in the hall and even another group in the kitchen. The bathroom floor was almost totally covered with the dead.

I stood in the living room and looked around. I couldn't believe the amount of death that was contained in such a small place. Nowhere was their just one corpse. There were always multiples. Now I just needed to determine what had happened since I wasn't home at the time. I didn't know who was responsible, but I needed to find out as whoever it was did a thorough job. It would be good to know who was capable of such professional work.

There weren't any cars in the driveway, but that

didn't tell me when Madge had left. The last time I had talked to her was about 9:30, and boy, was she steamed. Plenty of time for someone else to have arrived, done the job and left if she left not long after our conservation.

However, if she didn't leave until nearly noon the perpetrator would have had to get in, do the deed and get out really fast. Maybe when Madge gets home, if she does, all will become clear. In the mean time I have to decide what to do about the situation. I can't just leave dead bodies scattered around the house.

It didn't look like she was going to be home anytime soon so I decided it was up to me. She would be even madder if she came home and found out she also had to clean up. Having to take care of the situation herself was why she was so mad. Said all I ever did was put things off and then she had to do everything.

I took off my suit coat, loosened my tie, rolled up my shirtsleeves and reached for the broom. No doubt about it that guy had done a really good job. With a shrug I surrendered to the inevitable and began to sweep. After all, I couldn't leave dead roaches all over the floor. It really wasn't sanitary.

A Perfectly Good Explanation

Sheriff Don Wilson slowly circled the body of the man lying in the middle of what appeared to be the kitchen. Adjacent to his head, but about three feet away, lay an iron skillet with a large smear of blood on the back and up one side. Tangled around where the handle joined the base were several long strands of gray-black hair. Standing in the doorway flanked by two deputies was a short, rather dumpy woman dressed in a faded man's shirt about four sizes too big, worn flip-flops and baggy jeans with holes in both knees. It was pretty obvious her attire wasn't a fashion statement. Her shoulders were slumped and in her arms she cradled a large, long-haired black cat, obviously dead.

After photographing the scene from several angles and placing the skillet in a large bag he taped shut, Wilson finally addressed the waiting woman, still standing in the same place and slowly stroking the cat.

"And your name is?" Wilson asked.

For a moment there was no response. Then she raised her head. "Marcie Hawkins."

"And your relationship to the deceased?"

"His wife. Well I guess now I've been upgraded to widow."

Wilson attention became more sharply focused at this response. He wasn't sure if she was making a joke or just being very specific in her response to his question. In his fifteen years in law enforcement he had received a lot of different responses to his questions, but he couldn't remember anyone making a joke about committing murder.

"And what is your husband's full name?"

"Jefferson Ernest Hawkins. Now, ain't that a mouthful?"

"You want to tell me what happened?"

Marcie heaved a big sigh, tightened her grip on the cat and for the first time looked Wilson squarely in the eye. "Yeah, reckon I do."

"You understand you don't have to," Wilson said.

"I understand. The thing is, I don't know if you've really got time to hear it all."

"What do you mean?"

"I speck it's going to take a while. You don't come to doing something like this just all to once. You ponder on it quite a while and then something happens and you know it's the right time."

"Would you like to go in the other room and sit

down?"

"Nope, I'll stand right here. Might forget something it I weren't right here. Guess it be best if I start at the beginning."

When Wilson just nodded, Marcie took a deep breath, looked down at the cat and begun.

"Me and Jefferson, he always made me call him Jefferson, not Jeff. Said it showed more respect. Trouble was he never really done nothing to cause anybody to want to show him respect, but he swore it was due."

By this time both deputies and the ambulance crew waiting to get orders to remove the body were totally silent, hanging on her every word.

"We been married twenty-three years last month. I was fifteen and he just turned thirty. He done got me in the family way and my Dad said we was getting married like it or not. You just didn't tell my Dad "no" about nothing. Least wise not unless you really enjoyed a whipping, so I didn't argue. Besides, what other choice did I have? Maw weren't going to let me stay there. She already had seven young'uns younger than me and she sure didn't want to take on no grandkid. So, Dad talked the judge into letting us get married and he married us, too. Don't think he really wanted to, but I guess he didn't know no other way to go either."

"How many years have you been married?"

"As of last month, twenty.

"How many kids do you have and where are they?"

"Just the one; Jeff Jr. Nothing would do his Dad but he be named after him. That sounds like he were proud of him, but if he were he took a strange way to show it. Beat on him almost from day one every time Jeff made him mad and it don't taking nothing to make him mad."

"Where is Jeff now?"

"State prison; got caught robbing a drug store. Thought he could get rich selling dope."

"How old is he and how long has he been in prison?"

"He'll be twenty next month and he's been in almost five years. Couldn't behave his self in there either, so he got bridged, I think they call it, into the pen when he out-growed juvie."

Wilson stood quietly as Marcie seemed to be thinking something over. After a few minutes she continued.

"Beat me so bad I had Jeff early. He were only five pounds. Hurt me so bad the doctors had to operate. I guess it probably were a good thing they had to take all my baby-making insides. At least I only have one kid in jail."

"What brought on what happened today?"

"I were fixin' supper. Going to fry some taters with some bacon. Maybe open a can of beans and Rascal, this is Rascal." She stopped and indicated the cat she was still holding. "He smelled the bacon I guess. Anyhow, he jumped up on the table there near the stove and was leaning over trying to see what was on the cabinet. I had just set the skillet on the stove and was ready to put some lard in it when Jefferson just went nuts. He knocked me down, then grabbed Rascal and wrung his neck. Just like killing a chicken. When he threw him down and started to stomp on him I just grabbed that old skillet and hit him hard as I could. He done took everything else away from me. He weren't gonna' get away with killing my cat."

With great reluctance, Wilson placed handcuffs on Marcie's wrists. In his heart he felt justice had already been meted out.

As they went out the door, Marcie looked up at Wilson. "You'll see he gets buried right won't you? I mean Rascal, not Jefferson?"

"Yes, Marcie, I will," he responded. "I surely will.

At Last!

I sank down next to my life-long love and careful-
ly laid the .22 RG just above the top of his head. It
was hard to touch him, but I had to know for sure. His
skin was warm when I felt for the artery in his neck
and again when I held his hand and gently pressed his
wrist. There was no pulse.

I didn't realize I was crying until my glasses began
to blur. Removing them I used the tail of my shirt to
wipe both the glasses and my face dry. I had hardly
accomplished the task when the continuing flow
again blurred my sight.

"I'm so sorry," I said, gently brushing his hair
back so I could see all of his face. The blue eyes started straight at me, but I was sure this time they
weren't seeing me or anything else. Gone was the

teasing twinkle that he had aimed at me from as far back as I could remember. "I'm so sorry it had to end this way, but I just couldn't take another round."

I leaned back and wrapped my arms around my knees. For days I had been trying to decide. Ever since he told me he was going to marry again. Three times was just too many. My thoughts went back to the first time I could remember seeing him. I don't how long his family had lived across the street from us, I was only two at the time and he was four and his older brother six, but I know I still hadn't had my third birthday when they moved there. I know that because I still have the present he gave me for that event; a small, plush figure of a dog, apparently an attempt to replicate the story-book character Lassie, which I have, even though it's too worn to sleep with. I think that was the day I fell in love with him.

It's funny how life turns out. You think you know just how it is going to proceed and then you come home from high school and you mother tells you the family is invited to his wedding. His wedding! We had never even gone on a date! I never had a chance! She went on to say he was marrying a girl he had met at college and the wedding was to be at her home. The town was located about 50 miles away so we weren't going; too far, according to my dad.

Over the years I never faltered in my love. We saw each other a few times when he came to visit his folks and, after they died, to see his brother who had settled on the home place. Then one day I heard the news. His wife had died in a car wreck. My heart hurt for him, but at the same time hope was renewed. Less than a year later he married again. Another crushing blow, but less than two years later my hopes were again revived when she left him for the attorney that had handled her previous divorce. During that time I had given in and married another neighborhood boy who had professed his love for me from the time we were nine or ten. We got along fine until I heard about the divorce. As soon as possible I followed suite. I had to be ready when he at last realized I was the one that truly loved him. My husband never understood though I think he began to make the connection when I filed so soon after hearing the news about the other divorce

I leaned over and gently kissed the lips I had longed to kiss for so many years.

"I'm sorry," I whispered again. "I just couldn't take having my heart broken again. I know you never knew I thought of you other than as a friend. I tried to tell you so many times, but the words would just never come out. When I heard you were again planning to marry, and especially when I found out who you were marrying, I knew I had to do something. It wouldn't have been so bad, but she was the one that always beat me out of everything. She had better grades, got to do more things like take dance lessons, lived in a house big enough she had her own room while I shared with two sisters, got to go to college and I didn't. I just couldn't let her beat me this last time. You should have listened.

Again, I stroked his hair, leaned over, and kissed

him gently on the cheek. This is the last time something like that is going to keep us apart I told him. I
picked up the gun, placed it against my heart and
prepared to join my life-long love were nobody could
ever again come between us.

Fatal Address

"But that's the address you told me."

"Why would I tell you that address when she doesn't live there? Never did."

"I don't know. But I did what you said. Did a good job too."

I gave a deep sigh. It wouldn't do any good to argue with Mike. He never got anything right and never admitted he was the one in the wrong, but this time he had really outdone himself.

This whole thing started last week, Saturday night to be exac,t when we were watching the OU-OSU football teams go at it. This was the first game we watched together since my wife, Karen, and I split up, and Mike was doing a lot of telling me how lucky I was she was gone. No more having to pay the big casino bills she ran up, no more having to listen to her complaining about how little my job as a parole office paid, no more griping about the friends I had over to watch football, and on and on.

After while I sort of tuned him out and concentrated on the game. As OSU pulled farther and farther ahead it became less able to hold my attention.

"I'm telling you. You need to get rid of her once and for all,"

I looked over at Mike. He was dead serious.

"And just how am I supposed to do that?"

Mike gave me that sly grin that always preceded him making some pronouncement he deemed really intelligent.

"You could kill her."

"What!"

"Yeah, do her in."

"Where did you get an idea like that?"

Mike turned a hurt look in my direction. "From Listening to you. All you do is complain how mean she is. How she wastes money, how nothing you do is right. Things like that."

I turned his statement over in my mind. He was right. For once Mike was right. That was all I'd done these last two years. But kill her? Kill my wife? Well, ex-wife now. I thought about it some more. It would be nice not to have to wonder every time the phone rings if it was her and I was due to get another reaming out. Not to have bill collectors bugging me. They always seemed to think I was lying when I told them she didn't live here anymore. Even when I gave them her new address and phone number and wished them luck, but I suddenly realized what I wanted most of all was never having to listen to Mike tell me what all she'd done to me and what I should do about it. Sometimes it seemed as though he nagged me as bad she had.

"And just how would you propose I should do that?"

Mike stared at me for a minute. "Don't you have any ideas?"

"No, I hadn't really thought about it until you brought it up. Since it was your idea I figured you had it all planned out."

Mike scratched his head, squinted his eyes and rubbed his chin as though all that activity would kick his brain into gear and allow him to come up with a master plan.

"You could run her car off the road over by the bridge."

"Now, don't you think the cops would get suspicious real fast if my car came up with front-end damage at the same time she's run off the road?"

"Right, that won't work. Let me think?

After another session of rubbing and squinting, Mike again was ready to propose a plan.

"You could have her over and put rat poison in her coffee."

"And the police wouldn't be all over this place looking for the poison?"

I watched in amusement as Mike continued to irritate the small amount of brain he had by forcing his plans through it. Finally he stood up.

"I go to do some thinking. Why don't you? You're the one I'm trying to help?"

"I'm not the one that wants her dead. Besides I could just change my phone number. After the judge signs the divorce next week I'm no longer responsible for her bills. I can wait it out."

"Suit yourself, but I reckon you'd be better off if she was dead." With that parting shot he shoved open the door and stomped across the yard to where his truck was parked, front wheels in the flower bed as usual.

"I told you she was living in her folk's apartment over the garage not the apartment behind the garage. First you call me and tell me my problems are taken care of. I don't know what you're talking about, and then my Dad calls and says somebody broke in and killed the lady that was living there. You know Karen. How could you kill somebody else thinking it was her?"

"I didn't turn the light on."

I started at him in disbelief. If I had of had any idea he was serious maybe I could have stopped him, but he was always coming up with big plans to do something he thought would make him famous and never before had he attempted to follow though. And how the heck was I going to explain this to the police since I'm sure he's already told them he was doing me a favor? Well, this was the last time he was going to put me in some kinds of a predicament I hadn't asked for, but would have to be the one that affected.

I had had enough. Looking him straight in the eye, I walked over to the end table, opened the drawer, pulled out my .32 Rugger, pointed it at him, and shot him right between the eyes. Now, I was free of both problems and whatever came next couldn't be any worse. Maybe now I could get some peace. I laid the gun on the end table and dialed 911.

It Took Me a While, but I Never Forgot

Thank goodness the door was open. I don't know if my courage would have held out if I'd had to open a door not knowing who might be on the other side. As it was my feet felt glued to the floor just two steps from being inside the room. Cold sweat trickled down my face and for a minute I thought I wasn't going to be able to breathe. I had waited 30-years for this moment and now there was the distinct possibility I wouldn't be able to finish what I had so often dreamed of doing.

Feeling like my feet were being dragged down by quicksand, I finally managed to propel myself through the door and up within about six feet of a hospital bed. Lying on the bed was a shrunken figure of what used to be a man over six feet and nearly 200-pounds. He was attached to several tubes and wires

and from the looks of his skin still not getting enough
oxygen despite the feed to his nose that was continually providing the life-sustaining commodity. As I
stood there his eyes partially opened and after a
moment's hesitation I saw first recognition and then
fear spark in them. Good, he not only knew me he
knew why I was there.

As I stood there the years melted away and I was
again a seven-year-old standing on the bank above
the river, holding the hand of my sister who was four
and looking down on our father standing over the
body of a teen-age girl we had just recently picked up
as she hitchhiked toward the main highway. My sister
began to cry and this caused our father, I could never
think of him as "Daddy" from this time on, to look up
and see the two of us staring horrified at the picture
before us.

"Get the hell back in the truck," he screamed at
us. "I told you not to get out until I got back. Get in
the truck!"

His voice not only increased in volume, but, to
me anyway, in menace. I grabbed my sister's hand
and ran for the truck, partially dragging her as her
four-year-old legs weren't nearly as long as mine that
had three more years of growth to draw from. There
we huddled in the cab, my sister with her head buried
in my shoulder, her tears soaking my shirt, and me,
afraid to look and afraid not to. In a few minutes I saw
my father appear on the path that lead to the water's
edge carrying the girl like a limp sack of grain, slung
over his shoulder. He stopped at an old dug well near

what at one time was a yard surrounding a farm house, pushed aside the old boards that covered it, and dropped the girl into the hole. As quickly as possible he got back in the truck, glared at the two of us and before driving out of the field, continuing his original reason for being in the area, checking a series of oil wells to make sure they were working properly. He again glared at us and very slowly and deliberately said, "Keep your mouths shut!"

I moved a little closer to the bed and saw both the glare and the slight indication of fear increase. I had kept my mouth shut until about three years ago when I learned he had cancer. He and Mom had divorced years ago, but one of my sisters, not the one that was with me on that day, and I had stayed with him. He had promised me the ranch and the oil business if I would stay and help him run them. I don't know why I believed him. He made my life a living hell, caused me to treat Mom badly and totally destroyed my sister's ability to trust, cope, or believe in anything. After she tried to kill herself and her child, I decided it was time I spoke up. Mom didn't know what had happened that day, but knew something bad had. My sister and I were too different from then on.

Mom got on the internet and checked every place my father had lived from the time he was a teenager. At each location she discovered a record of missing or murdered women or teenage girls during the time he lived in the area. None of these had been solved and there were none just before or just after he left.

We went to the police, but since the only witnesses, my sister and I, were so young when it happened we couldn't remember exactly where the old well had been or the other locations where he had stopped the truck and left us while he went into the woods or down a creek bank with a girl, always returning alone. We never again followed him.

I took another step towards the bed. Even though I knew there was no way he could harm me now, it still was very hard to get any closer. He was sick, weak, shrunken and old and I was over six feet, not quite 200-pounds, and strong from years of oil field and agriculture work. Still I felt threatened.

As I looked at him, I couldn't help but blame myself for what had happened to many of those girls. I should have spoken up, taken the police to that old well when I could remember exactly where it was. I have no excuse except I was afraid. He had used his fists, boots and a belt on me too many times. When I was little, I remember trying so hard to please him, and nothing I ever did was good enough, done right, nor had anything about my effort that came up to his standards.

I moved a little closer to the bed and picked up his call button that was attached to the bottom bed sheet by a clip. Looking him straight in the eye, I unclipped the button and placed it just out of his reach. Then I picked up his oxygen tube and stood there holding it and staring straight into his eyes. Within seconds I knew he had gotten the message.

You have been nothing but evil all of your life, I told him moving that lifeline just out of his reach. Because of the way you treated my sisters they have led terrible lives. Because you made us think girls especially were supposed to be abused, all of them have been the victim many times. I wasted much of my life thinking if I just tried hard enough I could please you. Why I wanted to I don't really know. I guess it was partly because I was afraid if I didn't I'd wind up in the bottom of a well. You had me doubting myself, so I sometimes thought it really was because I was such a failure as a son that you were justified in treating me like you did. Well guess what, Dad. YOU WERE WRONG. I'm not a failure. I have a good business and people respect me and come to me for help and advice. You see, Dad, I worked in the oil field, but I also put myself through medical school. I'm now a physiatrist and people come to me asking for help to overcome mental problems. You have some of the worst mental problems I've ever seen. You think you are God and have the right to destroy anyone that doesn't do as you want. Well, I have a prescription for you that I think will take care of all of your problems from now on. After saying that I held the oxygen tube just inches out of his reach, squeezed it shut and listened to his final fight, which he lost.

Removing the surgical gloves I had been wearing and walking out the door without a backward glance, I felt the weight of all the years of abuse and secrets drop off like a tree shedding its leaves in a windstorm. By the time my truck doors closed behind me I had become a new man. Whatever happened next, the terrible burden I had carried most of my life was finally gone. With a smile I turned the ignition on and drove away, for the first time since I was a small child I actually enjoyed observing what was around me. Now I knew for sure he couldn't hurt me anymore.